First U.S. edition 2017

Library of Congress Catalog Card Number pending
ISBN 978-0-7636-8908-7

17 18 19 20 21 22 TLF 10 9 8 7 6 5 4 3 2 1

Printed in Dongguan, Guangdong, China.

This book was typeset in Adobe Garamond Pro, Gill Sans, and Adobe Caslon.
The illustrations were created in pencil and colored digitally.

TEMPLAR BOOKS

an imprint of
Candlewick Press
99 Dover Street
Somerville, Massachusetts 02144

www.candlewick.com

To Catherine
and Mikey

This is Max and Mia, and today is a VERY special day.

They trundle like elephants into the car

and cling like monkeys as Mom says good-bye.

They nibble like lemurs on some snacks on the bus.

And hide at the back of the line like scaredy meerkats.

It starts to get late . . .

and finally it's time to leave.

LEFT
BEHIND!

Luckily, Max is very good at being prepared.

And when the clock strikes midnight . . .

they make
a new friend!

They see flouncing flamingos
amid fabulous fountains . . .

and mischievous monkeys

in marvelous mountains,

Loud, laughing lemurs
with lanterns alight . . .

and pandas who prance through
pagodas all night.

They see kingly cats in
their comfortable keep . . .

and as the sun rises, they fall fast asleep.

When they wake up in the morning . . .

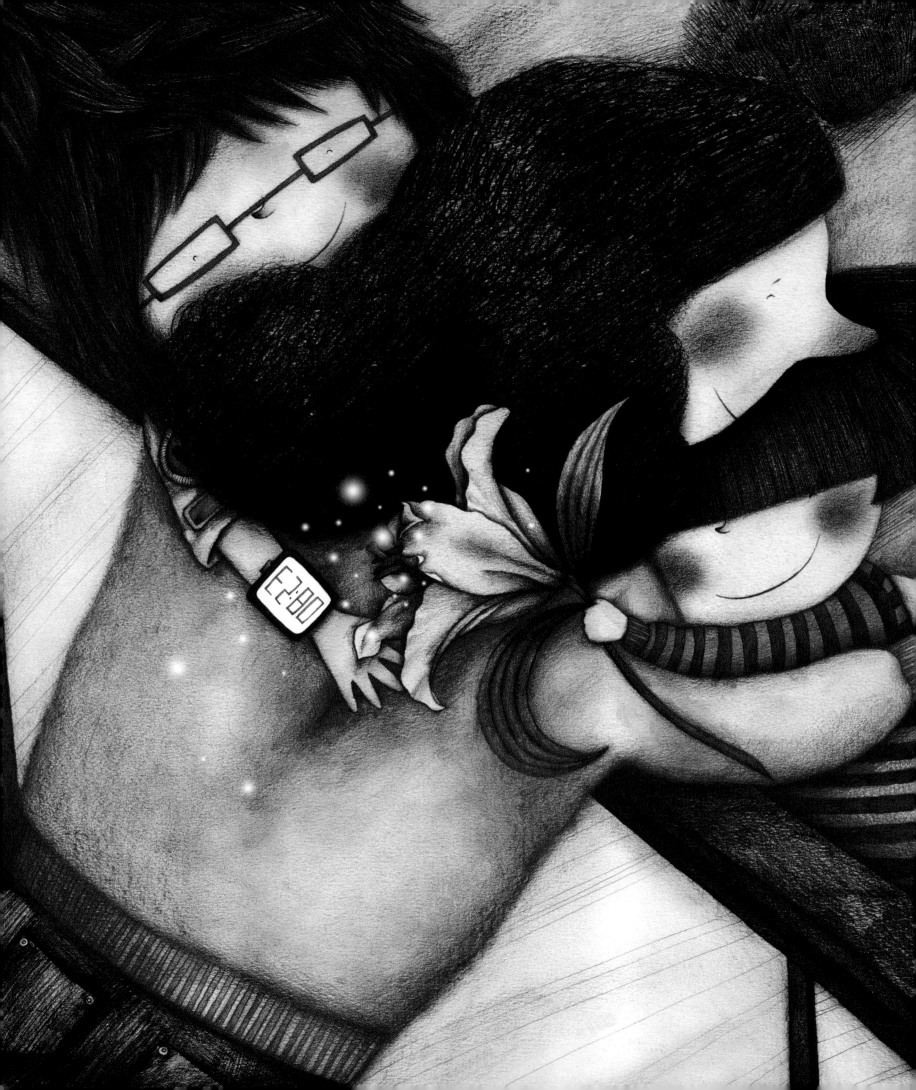

Mom hugs them tight,
and they tell about everything
they've seen overnight.

She doesn't believe them,
but we know it's true—
their magical visit
to the midnight zoo!